For Mark, James, Joe & Jess ~ J H

For Julia, Angus, Mitch, Cathy, Clay and
all the Stone crew . . . my lovely, inspiring
Aussie friends, thank you ~ C P

Copyright © 2009 by Good Books, Intercourse, PA 17534
International Standard Book Number: 978-1-56148-660-1
Library of Congress Catalog Card Number: 2008033191

Text copyright © Julia Hubery 2009
Illustrations copyright © Caroline Pedler 2009
Original edition published in English by Little Tiger Press,
an imprint of Magi Publications, London, England, 2009.

Printed in China

Library of Congress Cataloging-in-Publication Data

Hubery, Julia.

A friend like you / Julia Hubery ; illustrated by Caroline Pedler.

p. cm.

Summary: Best friends Panda and Monkey journey into the mountains to discover
its secrets, and Monkey learns from Panda how to appreciate beauty along the way.

ISBN 978-1-56148-660-1 (hardcover : alk. paper)

[1. Pandas--Fiction. 2. Monkeys--Fiction. 3. Jungle animals--Fiction. 4. Nature--Fiction.]
I. Pedler, Caroline, ill. II. Title.

PZ7.H863166Frn 2009

[E]--dc22

2008033191

A Friend Like You

Julia Hubery   Caroline Pedler

Good Books

Intercourse, PA 17534
800/762-7171
www.GoodBooks.com

Panda stretched happily in the morning sun. It was the first day of spring, time for his special journey up into the mountains.

Sunlight sparkled in the trees as Panda walked through the peaceful forest. Suddenly, a nut hit him on the nose. It was Monkey!

"Where are you going, Panda?" he giggled. "Anywhere fun?"

"Monkey, come and see this!" he called.
But Monkey was out of sight.
"Poor Monkey," thought Panda.
"In such a rush, he never sees anything!
I wonder where he's gone?"

Before long, Panda
found him chasing his
tail around a tree.
"You're taking forever," said Monkey,
"and I couldn't find the silly river!"
"If you hush a minute, you'll hear
it," said Panda. "We're almost there."

"But I'm too excited to hush!" laughed Monkey, chattering away as they strolled on together.

Soon they reached
the banks of Silver River.
"I'm going to swing across,"
boasted Monkey. "Watch me fly, Panda!"
"Be careful!" Panda called out, as
Monkey leapt up into the branches.

Panda swam slowly down into the cool
water, smiling as a shoal of flickering
fish tickled by his toes.

Monkey came swinging
through the treetops.
 "I'll beat you across,
old soggy-ploddy-bear!"
he shouted.

"One,
two,
three,
whheeeeee,
look at
meeeeee!"

Monkey let go of his branch
and soared up, up through
the glorious sky . . .

. . . then down,

Splash!

into the river.

"Help!" he shrieked.

"Here I am," shouted Panda. "Hold on tight!"
He pulled the squidgy, shivering monkey
from the water and swam to the shore.

"Poor little monkey-mess! However did
I find a friend like you?" Panda laughed.
"Come on – have a ride on my back!"
Monkey snuggled into Panda's cozy
fur. "Thank you, Panda," he whispered.

Up and up Panda climbed through the misty foothills.

"Monkey, did you ever see anything so pretty?" he gasped, but there was no answer. Monkey was fast asleep.

"Sleep well, little friend," Panda whispered, and padded softly on.

At last they reached the lush, green meadows.
"Are we there yet?" squeaked Monkey,
bouncing awake. "Can I see the secret now?"
"It's up in the highest meadow," said Panda.
"The mountain butterflies are about to fly -
it's an amazing sight!"

"Quick, I want to see them!"
Monkey squealed.

"Wait!" called Panda. "I can't keep up."

"But they'll fly away!" Monkey cried,
skipping off. Panda sighed sadly and
climbed slowly after him.

When Panda reached the top, Monkey was looking very cross. "There aren't any butterflies!" he snapped. "We've missed them, all because you're such a slowpoke!"

"That's not very fair," cried Panda. "I can't rush like you. It's just the way I am."

Panda padded on in the leafy shade. As he stopped to chew some bamboo, he heard a chirrup under the leaves. There he found a colorful bird, bright as a jewel.

"Somewhere with a beautiful secret," said Panda. "Do you want to come too?"

"Yes, please!" squealed Monkey. "I love secrets!"

As they set off, Monkey danced around Panda, hurrying him along. "Come on," he squeaked. "I want to see the secret!"

"Slow down, little friend," said Panda. "It's a long way. We have to cross Silver River first, then follow the rocky stream to the mountain meadows."

"That sounds easy," said Monkey. "Let's get going, Panda-plod!" And he raced ahead.

Monkey hung his head. "I'm sorry, Panda," he said.
"I know I'm lucky to have a friend like you."

Panda smiled. "Don't worry, little Monkey,"
he said gently. "All we have to do now is wait –
ever so quiet, and ever so still."

Monkey snuggled next to Panda, and slowly,
slowly, slowly . . .

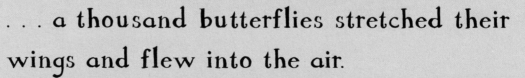

. . . a thousand butterflies stretched their
wings and flew into the air.

"They're amazing!" Monkey whispered.
"Thank you, Panda."

Panda hugged him and smiled. "I'm happy
I can share them with a friend like you."